Pony-Crazed Princess

Princess Ellie's Secret

Read all the adventures of Princess Ellie!

#1 Princess Ellie to the Rescue
#2 Princess Ellie's Secret
#3 Princess Ellie's Mystery

Pony-Crazed Princess

Princess Ellie's Secret

by Diana Kimpton

Illustrated by Lizzie Finlay

Hyperion Paperbacks for Children
New York

For Jack

First published in the United Kingdom in 2004 as
The Pony-Mad Princess: Princess Ellie's Secret
by Usborne Publishing Ltd.
Based on an original concept by Anne Finnis
Text copyright © 2004 by Diana Kimpton and Anne Finnis
Illustrations copyright © 2004 by Lizzie Finlay

Printed in the United States of America
First U.S. edition, 2006
1 3 5 7 9 10 8 6 4 2

This book is set in 14.5-point Nadine Normal.

ISBN 0-7868-4871-5

Visit hyperionbooksforchildren.com

Chapter 1

"Steady, Shadow," said Princess Ellie. The black Shetland pony she was riding pawed at the ground with his tiny front hoof. He was eager to start the relay race and couldn't understand the delay.

"Are you all right all the way down there?" asked Kate, with a grin. She was riding Sundance, Ellie's chestnut pony, who was much taller than Shadow.

Ellie grinned back. "Just you wait," she said. "Sometimes it's good to be small." She was so glad Kate had come to live with her grandparents, who worked at the palace. It was good to have a friend at last, and they had a lot of fun together with Ellie's four ponies.

"Are you two ready?" called Meg, the palace groom. When they both nodded, she shouted, "One, two, three, go."

The two ponies leaped forward and galloped across the field toward two piles of clothes on the other side. Ellie leaned forward, urging Shadow on. But the Shetland, with his short legs, was no match for Sundance. The chestnut pony pulled ahead;

he reached Kate's pile of clothes first.

Oh, no, thought Ellie, as she saw Kate leap off Sundance and start putting on a long, floppy coat.

Shadow finally reached the other pile, and Ellie had to concentrate on her own part in the race.

Jumping off Shadow was easy—Ellie's feet were nearly touching the ground anyway. Then she pulled on a long coat, wrapped a scarf around her neck, and crammed a wide-brimmed hat on top of her pink-and-gold riding helmet.

She glanced over at Kate, expecting to see her making her way back. But she wasn't. She was struggling to mount Sundance. Now that she was dressed up it was hard for her to lift her foot high enough to reach the stirrup.

"We've still got a chance, Shadow," cried Ellie. She didn't have Kate's problem. Shadow was so small that she was able to jump into the saddle without even using the stirrups.

She urged the Shetland into a gallop and headed back toward the finish line. Soon she could hear Sundance's hooves pounding after them, but this time the lead was too great. Shadow raced across the line just ahead of the chestnut pony.

"Ellie's the winner," shouted Meg.

"Well done," said Kate. "Being small was definitely an advantage that time."

Suddenly, a voice called out, "Princess Aurelia!"

Ellie looked around and saw Miss

Stringle standing at the end of the field near the palace. Miss Stringle always insisted on using Ellie's full name. To Ellie's annoyance, so did nearly everyone else in the royal household, especially the King and Queen. Ellie trotted Shadow across the field to say hello. But as soon as she was close enough to see her governess's face, she realized something was wrong.

"Whatever are you doing, Your Royal Highness?" asked Miss Stringle, giving Ellie one of her disapproving looks.

Ellie ignored the look and cheerfully replied, "We're playing mounted games. You know, when we use the ponies to help. I just won. Did you see?"

"Indeed I did," declared Miss Stringle. "And I'm horrified to see you making such an exhibition of yourself. It is not suitable behavior for a princess."

Ellie felt confused. What, she wondered, was wrong with winning a race? Then she remembered the hat, coat, and scarf. "I had to wear these," she explained, as she pulled off the hat. "You can't be in this type of relay race without dressing up."

"I am not talking about the clothes," said Miss Stringle. "It's the pony that's the problem. It's much too small." As she spoke, she waved her hand at Shadow. The greedy Shetland instantly assumed he was being offered food. He stuck out his nose and nuzzled Miss Stringle's outstretched palm. She pulled her hand away quickly and dabbed it clean with a lace-trimmed hankie.

Normally, Ellie would have been tempted

to laugh. But this time, she was too angry. "Shadow's not too small," she said. "He's exactly the right size for a Shetland."

"But that's not the right size for *you*," said Miss Stringle. "You look ridiculous. I'll have to tell your parents." Without waiting for Ellie to reply, she marched back to the palace with a determined look on her face.

Ellie's heart sank. Deep down inside, she knew Miss Stringle was right.

Shadow was her first pony, and she could hardly remember a time when he hadn't been there for her to love. He'd been her birthday present the year she was four, and he'd been just the right size for her then. But over the years, she had grown, and he hadn't.

Now her feet nearly touched the ground when she was riding him. She had hoped no one else would notice. But now someone had. What would happen to Shadow if she couldn't ride him anymore?

Chapter 2

Ellie didn't have to wonder for very long. By the time she and Kate had ridden back to the stable, the King and Queen were already there. They looked out of place in their royal clothes and everyday crowns. Their long velvet robes trimmed with ermine definitely had not been designed with straw and manure in mind.

Miss Stringle was with them. She pointed

at Ellie as she rode up on Shadow. "You see what I mean, Your Majesty. The princess looks ridiculous."

The King stifled a laugh. "She's quite right, Aurelia. Shadow's much too small for you now."

"But I love him," said Ellie. "We've been together for ever and ever. And I don't mind what I look like."

"But we do," said the Queen. "Princesses must always look dignified. You really should not ride him anymore."

"Perhaps Kate could instead," suggested Ellie. "She's not a princess, so you can't care what she looks like." To Ellie's delight, Kate enthusiastically agreed. Perhaps this was the solution.

But the Queen smiled and shook her head. "That's a nice idea, but Kate's legs are even longer than yours. And, this isn't just about appearances. It's about what's right for Shadow."

"The fact of the matter is that you are *both* too big to ride him," said the King firmly. Then he turned to Meg and added, "Please arrange for the pony to be sold."

Ellie was too shocked to speak. Not being able to ride Shadow was bad enough. Losing him would be unbearable.

Meg saw Ellie's dismay. "Don't worry," she said reassuringly. "We'll find him a really good home."

Ellie jumped down and stood defensively between Shadow and the adults. "He doesn't need a good home," she said, angrily. "He's got a good home already." Shadow nuzzled her pocket for a treat, unaware that his future hung in the balance.

The Queen put her arm around Ellie's shoulders. "I'm sure you'll get used to the idea, Aurelia."

"And you will still have Sundance, Rainbow, and Moonbeam," added the King. "Surely, three ponies are enough for anyone." He turned to leave. The conversation was over.

Ellie watched miserably as her parents walked back to the palace with Miss Stringle. How could they be so mean? Didn't they understand how much she loved Shadow?

Sundance seemed to sense that something was wrong. He reached out his chestnut head and blew gently down his nose at the Shetland. The two ponies had been friends since they first met. They often stayed together in the field, standing head to tail to protect each other from the flies.

Ellie stroked Sundance's chestnut nose. "You'll miss Shadow, too, won't you?"

"So will I," said Kate, as she ran her fingers through the Shetland's black mane. Then she glanced at Ellie and added, "It must be much harder for you."

Ellie flung her arms around Shadow's neck. "It won't feel like home without him. He's always been here. George taught me to ride on him."

Kate looked confused. "Was George the groom before Meg?" she asked. "The one who wouldn't let you help look after your ponies?"

"Yes," said Ellie, as she gave the Shetland the treat he'd been looking for. She was glad George had retired. It had given her time to get to know the ponies—all of them.

Suddenly, she had an idea. There was no time to lose. "Hold these," she yelled, shoving Shadow's reins into Kate's hands and racing after her parents and Miss Stringle.

They were already way ahead of her, so she took a shortcut, leaping over a low bush and running across the neatly manicured lawn. The King and Queen were just walking up the gravel path to the magnificent main entrance when Ellie squeezed between two large rosebushes and ran out in front of them. Miss Stringle's eyebrows shot straight up at the sight of such unprincesslike behavior, but Ellie didn't have time to apologize.

"I've got a great idea," she said. "We don't need to get rid of Shadow after all."

The King and Queen looked doubtful, so Ellie continued quickly, before they could stop her. "He's worked really hard for years, just like George did. So couldn't he retire and be happy, like George? Then it wouldn't matter that there's no one to ride him. He could just stay here and spend the rest of his life eating grass and doing nothing."

"Hmmm," said the King, thoughtfully. "I can't see anything wrong with that."

The Queen smiled. "It sounds like a perfect solution. You'd better go back and tell Meg we won't be selling Shadow." She glanced sideways at Miss Stringle and added, "But this time, please use the path."

Ellie was so delighted that she gave her mom a big hug. Then she headed back to the stable, trying to walk in as dignified a way as possible until the royal party went inside. As soon as she was sure they couldn't see her anymore, she started to run as fast as she could.

She found the others in the tack room

and blurted out her news. Kate was as happy as she was, but, to Ellie's surprise, Meg seemed less excited.

"What's wrong?" Ellie asked her. "I thought you liked Shadow."

Meg shook her head and smiled. "Of course I do. I'm just worried that retirement might not be the best thing for him."

Ellie walked away from the tack room. She didn't want to hear Meg's doubts. She was sure her plan was perfect. What could possibly go wrong?

Chapter 3

The next day, Ellie was in the middle of a boring math lesson when a footman arrived. Miss Stringle glared at him. The classroom was her territory, and she didn't like being interrupted.

The footman ignored her glare. He straightened the jacket of his red-and-gold uniform, pulled himself up to his full height, and announced, "Their Majesties, the King and Queen, wish to see Princess Aurelia immediately in the parlor."

Even Miss Stringle couldn't ignore such an important summons. She snapped her book shut and waved Ellie toward the door. "You'd better go," she said. "But make sure you come straight back."

Ellie was delighted to escape. She was happy to take a break from math, and she loved going to the parlor. She was fascinated by the dozens of animals galloping across the painted ceiling, but there was no time to look at those today. The King and Queen stood by one of the tall windows, waiting for Ellie. Meg was with them, and so was the royal vet. They all looked very serious.

Ellie's mouth went dry with fear. This was not a good sign. Something must be wrong. Had there been an accident? Was one of her ponies hurt?

"We've been talking about Shadow," said the King.

"Is he sick?" asked Ellie, her fear growing worse by the minute.

"No, he isn't sick," said the Queen. "But Meg *is* worried about him. She thinks retiring Shadow is a bad idea."

"No, it's not," argued Ellie. "He'll love doing nothing. He'll be able to stand in the field and eat all day long."

"That's the problem," said Meg. "Too *much* food and too *little* exercise will make Shadow very fat."

Ellie scowled at her. "What's wrong with that?" she snapped. She felt betrayed. Meg was usually on her side.

The King stepped between them. "Calm down, Aurelia," he said, firmly. "Being rude won't get you anywhere. We're only trying to do what's right for Shadow."

"It doesn't feel like it," Ellie muttered under her breath. She tried hard to look calm

21

although she didn't feel calm inside.

The vet smiled. "Shadow is a wonderful pony," he said. "I can see why you love him so much."

Ellie felt a glimmer of hope and gave him a small smile back. Maybe there was someone on her side after all.

The vet walked over to the fireplace and turned to face them, his hands behind his back. "The problem is that Shadow's a Shetland pony," he continued. "That breed is designed to work hard on not much food. If he does nothing but eat all day, he could get very sick."

"Like a tummy-ache?" asked Ellie, remembering the last time she had eaten too much chocolate cake.

"No, worse," said Meg with a sigh. "He could get laminitis."

"What's that?" Ellie asked. She had seen that term in her pony books, but she had never understood what it was.

"It's an illness that overfed ponies can get," explained the vet. "It makes the insides of their feet hot and inflamed. It's very painful, and it can damage their feet so badly that they never get better."

"That's why I'm worried about Shadow," said Meg. "If he got laminitis, he'd really suffer. He would be one sad pony."

The Queen walked forward and put a sympathetic arm around Ellie's shoulders. "So, can you see that retirement isn't right for Shadow, Aurelia?" she asked.

"Yes," said Ellie miserably, as her glimmer of hope disappeared. The idea hadn't been so perfect after all. She'd have felt awful if Shadow had gotten sick.

"I'm glad that's settled," announced the King. "Meg will arrange to sell him as soon as possible."

Ellie started to cry. "Please don't make him go," she begged. "I'll do anything. Just let Shadow stay."

"No amount of tears or begging is going to make me change my mind," said the King firmly. "Shadow needs plenty of exercise, and the only place he's going to get that is in a new home."

Ellie knew her father wouldn't change his mind. But she couldn't stand the thought of losing Shadow.

This was turning into the worst day of Ellie's life . . . ever.

Chapter 4

Ellie found it hard to concentrate when she got back to the classroom. Her brain was too busy trying to think up a way to keep Shadow. Miss Stringle interrupted her thoughts by tapping Ellie's desk with a ruler. "So, what is the answer, Your Highness?" she asked, impatiently.

"I'm not sure," muttered Ellie. That was an understatement. She didn't even know what the question was.

"Think carefully," said Miss Stringle in an exasperated tone. "If there are twelve princesses and nine princes, how many couples can live happily ever after?"

"Twelve?" guessed Ellie.

Miss Stringle raised her eyebrows.

"Eleven?" said Ellie, watching the eyebrows closely. They didn't drop, so she tried again. "Nine?"

"At last," said Miss Stringle with a sigh of relief. "Arithmetic is obviously not your strong suit today. I think we should move on to some history."

"Do I have to?" asked Ellie without enthusiasm.

"Of course you do," replied Miss Stringle. "You're a princess. You must learn about your heritage." She pulled a huge book down from a shelf and placed it on Ellie's desk. "Maybe this will help get you interested."

To her surprise, Ellie saw that it was an old photograph album. Its red-leather cover was embossed with the royal coat of arms and a golden crown.

"Look inside," Miss Stringle told her. "There are pictures of the entire royal family, starting with the time when photography was invented."

Ellie slowly turned the pages. This was

much more interesting than learning the dates of ancient battles. "Look, that woman's wearing Mom's crown," Ellie said, pointing at a photo of a queen.

"That's your great-grandmother Queen Elspeth," said Miss Stringle. "She had that crown made for her. She said the old one gave her a headache."

Ellie laughed and looked at the next photo. She had to hold back another burst of laughter. The photo showed the grumpiest-looking king she had ever seen.

"That's her husband—your great-grandfather," explained Miss Stringle.

"He looks very mad," said

Ellie. "Maybe his crown gave him a headache, too." She turned to the next page, where two girls in frilly dresses and wide-brimmed hats smiled out at her from a picture.

"That's your grandmother and your great-aunt Edwina when they were little girls," explained Miss Stringle. She pointed at a stern lady standing near them. "And that's their governess. Doesn't she look elegant?

Governesses were so respected in those days." She paused and sighed wistfully.

But Ellie wasn't listening. She didn't care who the people in the photo were. What was much more important was that they were sitting in a carriage, and that that carriage was being pulled by a Shetland pony—just like Shadow. Maybe this was the answer to her problem. If Shadow learned to pull a carriage, it would keep him busy and give him plenty of exercise. Plus, she was sure that she and Kate would love driving him around the palace grounds.

The more Ellie thought about the idea, the more she liked it. By lunchtime, she was convinced she had discovered the perfect solution to the Shadow problem. She was excited at the thought of telling her parents the good news, but when she rushed into the dining room, they were busy talking. They looked up briefly and smiled. Then they ignored her and started talking to each other again.

Ellie considered interrupting, but decided against it when she realized they were talking about taxes. Although *she* found that one of the most boring topics in the world, her parents thought it was fascinating. They definitely wouldn't like being interrupted, and Ellie needed them to be in a good mood when they listened to her plan.

She wandered across the room to choose something to eat from the silver dishes laid out on the side table. The selection of food was mouthwatering. There were meats and fish of every kind, tomatoes cut into the shapes of lilies, delicate curls of cucumber, and warm rolls. Ellie was careful not to let the butler give her too much. She wanted to leave room for the desserts, which were piled temptingly on a nearby crystal dish.

She was just finishing the last bite of her salmon when the King and Queen finally stopped talking. The Queen smiled at Ellie and asked, "Are you feeling better, dear? You looked so upset after our little talk earlier."

Ellie smiled back. "I'm fine now," she said. "I've had . . ."

"Good," interrupted the King before Ellie could finish. "I'm glad you've realized that it's right to sell Shadow."

"No, no," cried Ellie. "We don't need to sell him. I've had the most wonderful idea."

"Not another one," said the King, sighing.

"This one's much better," said Ellie. "All we have to do is . . ."

"No," the King said firmly. "We've made up our minds. We must do what's right for Shadow, and that means finding him a new home. Someone is coming to pick him up at the end of next week."

Ellie turned desperately to her mother for help. "Please listen," she begged the Queen.

"This idea's perfect. I know it is."

But the Queen was just as tough as the King. "I'm sorry, Aurelia, but it's already been arranged. There is absolutely no point in arguing."

Ellie burst into tears and ran out of the room. She didn't even glance at the desserts left uneaten on the side table. She was too upset!

But she wasn't going to give up. She was sure her idea would work. She just had to prove it.

Chapter 5

Ellie was relieved when Kate came home from school later that day. She needed to talk to someone who would listen—someone who would take her side and help her keep Shadow.

They sat together in Ellie's bedroom while she told Kate the events of the day.

Ellie's bedroom was the pinkest room in the entire world. The King had designed it, and he was sure all princesses liked pink. Unfortunately, Ellie didn't. So, to cover up the pink, she had put up tons of pony posters and pictures of her own ponies. In her opinion, the room looked much better that way.

Kate squealed with delight when she heard Ellie's idea about teaching Shadow to pull a carriage. "That's a great plan!" she said. "It solves everything."

Ellie sighed. "It would if my mom and dad would let us do it."

"You'll just have to persuade them," said Kate.

"How can I?" groaned Ellie. "They won't even listen."

Kate sat on the rose-pink carpet and looked up at the pony posters that covered the pink-and-white-striped wallpaper. "Maybe you could show them the photo," she suggested. "The one that gave you the idea in the first place."

Ellie's face brightened and then grew thoughtful. "I don't think they'd look at a picture. But what if we taught Shadow to pull a carriage? Then we could show them the real thing and prove that my idea would work!" She paused for a moment. "We'll have to do it in secret," she added. "We don't want them to stop us."

"Good idea," said Kate. "I love secrets. So, what do we have to do?"

"I'm not sure," said Ellie. "But we can find out." She grabbed her *Encyclopedia of Horses*, found the right page, and started reading. But her excitement soon turned to dismay. "It says here that it takes at least six weeks to teach a pony how to pull a carriage."

"That's not good," said Kate. "He'll be gone in less than two."

"I know," moaned Ellie. "There isn't enough time."

They both stared sadly at the book. Then Ellie suggested they go for a ride. "It'll cheer us up," she said. "And maybe it will help us think more clearly."

Kate nodded in agreement, and they went to get Moonbeam and Rainbow from the  field. Then they put them in their stalls and went to get the brush box.

"Shut the door quickly," yelled Meg, as they stepped inside the tack room. A gust of wind had lifted up the pile of papers she was reading and blown them all over the place.

"Sorry," said Ellie, as she helped to pick them up.

"I'm looking for Shadow's paperwork," Meg explained. Then she saw the sad look on Ellie's face and added, "I'm sorry, but I have to do what I'm told. And it is the best thing for Shadow."

Ellie stared at the paper she was clutching in her hand.

"I think this is what you want," she said sadly, holding it out to Meg. "What does 'R and D' mean?"

Meg looked down at the paper in surprise. "It's short for 'ride and drive.'"

BILL OF SALE

Supplied to HRH King Conrad
by the Finnisbarne
Shetland Pony Stud:
One six-year-old
Shetland pony.

Registered Name:
Shadow of Finnisbarne.
R and D.
Complete with tack.

"And what exactly does that mean?" asked Kate.

Meg smiled. "It means you can either ride Shadow or you can harness him to a carriage and drive him."

Ellie stared at her in disbelief. "So Shadow knows how to pull a carriage?"

"Definitely," said Meg. "And to think, all this time, none of us knew."

"Wow!" cried Ellie triumphantly. She had a huge grin on her face as she added, "Maybe our plan will work after all."

Meg looked at the princess suspiciously. "What are you two up to?" she asked.

Ellie hesitated. It was Meg who had stopped her plan to retire Shadow. Would she stop this one, too?

Meg must have guessed what she was thinking. "Don't worry," she said. "I won't tell anyone your secret unless it's going to put you or Shadow in danger."

"Thanks," said Ellie, and launched into an excited explanation of her idea and how there wasn't enough time to teach Shadow. "But since he already knows how to pull a carriage, everything will be much easier," she finished in a rush.

"Remember, he hasn't done it in a long time," said Meg. "He'll need a quick refresher course. And we'll need to get him a set of the right–size driving harness *and* something for him to pull."

"Ellie, could you get your parents to buy them for you?" asked Kate.

"It's too risky," Ellie replied. "If I tell them about our plan, I'm sure they'll try to stop me."

Meg looked again at Shadow's bill of sale. "It says here that Shadow came complete with tack. I'm sure I've seen a harness around here somewhere. I wonder if it's his." She started burrowing through a pile of blankets in the far corner of the tack room.

Ellie and Kate rushed over to help her look.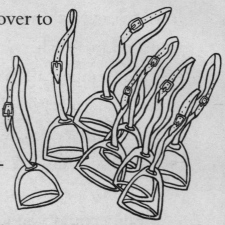

"There's so much stuff," said Kate, as she opened a cabinet and a pile of old stirrups tumbled out.

"I know," said Ellie, pushing some reins off a bench. "I don't think George liked throwing things away."

Suddenly, Ellie noticed that one of the bench tops had hinges. There must be a storage box underneath, she thought. She threw open the lid and peered inside. To her delight, she found a black leather harness that looked just the right size for Shadow.

"That's solved one problem, anyway," announced Kate. "We have the right tack."

"But we still need a carriage," sighed Ellie.

Meg took the harness from her and smiled. "Don't bother about that now. Go and have your ride. Moonbeam and Rainbow must be wondering what's happened to you two."

The girls knew better than to argue. They dashed out to tack up their ponies.

The pleasure of riding soon pushed Ellie's worries about Shadow to the back of her mind. She and Kate rode up through the woods, exploring the twisting paths and jumping over fallen logs. When they reached the open hilltop, they had a long canter across a field. Then they stopped to give the ponies a rest.

Kate looked down at the palace. "What are those buildings at the back?" she asked. "I've never noticed them before."

"They're just used for storing things," explained Ellie. "We hardly ever get rid of anything. Being royal means our old stuff isn't junk—it's history." Then she remembered the carriage in the photo. Was there a chance that it still existed?

Chapter 6

Ellie and Kate rode back to the palace as quickly as they could. They wanted to search the storage buildings right away, but there wasn't time before dinner. Luckily, the King and Queen had gone to a banquet in town. That meant there was no formal meal for Ellie to sit through. Instead, she had dinner with Miss Stringle and ate as quickly as she could without being accused of bad manners. As soon as she had finished, Ellie said she had a headache and persuaded Miss Stringle to let her go to her room to watch TV. But instead of going to her room, Ellie slipped outside to meet Kate.

Kate was waiting at the kitchen door with a couple of flashlights. "Are you sure it's a good idea to look now?" she asked nervously. "It'll be dark soon."

Ellie felt nervous, too, but she tried not to let it show. "We can't wait!" she said. "We're running out of time."

The storage buildings seemed bigger close up. They also looked dark and pretty neglected. Ellie had never gone inside before. There were probably spiders and maybe bats and mice as well. For a moment, she was overcome by fear, and wondered if they should give up the whole idea. Then she thought of Shadow and knew she had to keep going. She took a deep breath to calm herself and walked up to a large, wooden door.

"Won't it be locked?" said Kate. She sounded as if she'd be happy if it were.

"Not necessarily," said Ellie. "It's not like we put the crown jewels in here." She grabbed hold of the handle, turned it, and pulled. The door creaked open on its rusty hinges.

The two girls crept inside. In the dim light from the dirty windows, they could see stacks of boxes, crates, and strangely shaped objects covered with drop cloths.

"I don't think anyone's been in here for years," said Ellie.

"This stuff must be really old, then," said Kate, peering under the nearest drop cloth. The suit of armor underneath wobbled pre- cariously and then crashed to the ground. The loud noise made both girls jump. It echoed around the building, sounding extra loud in the surrounding silence of the dark room.

"Eeek!" shrieked Kate, when a mouse shot out of the helmet. It scuttled across the floor and disappeared.

Ellie followed the rodent. "That's more the size of what we're looking for," she said.

"What? The mouse?" asked Kate, horrified.

"Don't be silly," said Ellie. "I'm talking about the thing it's hiding behind."

She lifted the drop cloth and felt a thrill of excitement as she spotted a large wooden wheel. "Come on," she called, and wriggled underneath the cloth for a better look.

Kate followed her, and they both switched on their flashlights. But they didn't find a carriage. Instead, the wheel was attached to a strange, wooden hut.

"What on earth is
it?" asked Kate.

"I think it's for get-
ting changed in at the
beach," said Ellie, who
had seen something like it in a history book.

"I suppose your ancestors were way too
fancy and royal to wrap themselves up in a
plain old towel like everyone else," laughed
Kate.

She wanted to look inside, but Ellie
dragged her away. "We don't have time," she
said. "That's way too big for Shadow to pull.

We've got to keep look-
ing."

They searched and
searched in the fading
light. But the only other

thing they found with wheels was a strange-looking baby carriage. Eventually, Kate looked at her watch by the light of her flashlight. "I'll have to go soon or my grandma will get worried."

Ellie knew she had to go, too. "Just five more minutes," she said, pointing to a pile of packing cases. "We haven't looked behind those yet."

They ran around to the end of the pile and peered into the gloom. Right in front of them was something big, its shape hidden by another drop cloth. Ellie ran forward and looked under the edge of the cloth. "There's a wheel," she yelled. Kate joined her, and together they pulled the cloth on to the ground.

They gave a whoop of delight. Standing

before them was the pony carriage. It didn't look quite as nice as the one in the picture. The paint was peeling in places, and the cushions were filthy. But it was there!

Kate lifted up one of the shafts and tried to pull the carriage. Nothing happened. She pulled harder. Still nothing.

"Oh, no!" cried Ellie. "It has to work." She grabbed hold of the other shaft. "One, two, three, go," she yelled.

The two girls pulled as hard as they could. But it made no difference. The wheels were completely stuck.

Chapter 7

Ellie could barely sleep that night. Kate had said her granddad would be able to make the carriage move. Ellie knew he was really good at fixing things, but what if the wheels were stuck so firmly that even *he* couldn't move them? What would they do then?

In the morning, she climbed out of bed feeling tired and sad. But she cheered up a little when she remembered that it was

Saturday and the start of a vacation from classes. Miss Stringle thought days off were a waste of time, but Ellie didn't. What was the point in being a princess if she had to do lessons when all the other children in the kingdom were having fun? Since Kate's arrival at the palace, Ellie had insisted on having the same breaks as her friend. Now she was really glad that she had. With only a few days left to save Shadow, she had no time to waste.

As soon as breakfast was over, she ran to her room and pulled on a pale, pink fleece and her rose-pink jeans. Then she tugged on her boots and raced downstairs toward the stable, wishing her father would buy her clothes that weren't pink. In the hall, she nearly collided with the King and Queen, who were walking along reading a letter.

They looked very unhappy.

"What's wrong?" asked Ellie.

"It's your great-aunt Edwina," said the Queen with a sigh.

"Is she ill?" asked Ellie.

The King shook his head sadly. "No," he said. "It's worse than that. She's feeling great and coming to stay on Wednesday."

Now Ellie knew why her parents looked upset. Great-Aunt Edwina was an extremely difficult guest. Nothing was ever good enough, and she constantly complained that everything had been *so much better* when she was a girl.

"It's a good thing you insisted on getting that vacation," said the Queen. "You'll be able to help us entertain her."

Ellie opened her mouth to say she was too busy. Then she shut it again quickly, before any words came out. She couldn't risk giving away her secret now. But she needed every minute she could find to save Shadow. There was no time to spare for Great-Aunt Edwina.

Kate was waiting impatiently for her in the stable. She was nearly bursting with excitement. "He's done it," she yelled.

"Who's done what?" asked Ellie.

"My granddad," replied Kate. "He moved the carriage all the way to his workshop. It only needed some grease on the wheels to help them turn."

Ellie felt a twinge of disappointment that she hadn't been there to watch. But that was immediately replaced by her happiness at the good news. Kate said her granddad was going to meet them later to show them how to make the carriage as good as new.

In the meantime, they would concentrate all their efforts on Shadow. They brushed him carefully. Then they led him to the riding ring, where Meg showed them how to put on the harness.

"What are those?" asked Ellie, pointing to some pieces of leather beside Shadow's eyes.

"They're blinkers," explained Meg. "They stop him from seeing the carriage behind him." She threaded the reins through some rings on a pad on Shadow's back and passed them to Ellie. "It's time to get started," she said.

"Don't we need these?" asked Kate, pointing at some straps Meg had left hanging on the fence.

"Not today," said Meg. "We won't need them until he starts to pull something."

Ellie stood behind Shadow wondering how to make him move. If she were riding him, she would squeeze him with her legs, but she couldn't do that from the ground.

"Use your voice," Meg suggested.

"Walk on," called Ellie and, to her surprise, Shadow immediately stepped forward, turning his ears toward her as he waited for the next instruction.

Ellie pulled gently on the reins and said, "Whoa," firmly. Shadow stopped.

"That's amazing," said Kate.

Ellie told Shadow to walk on again, and they practiced twisting and turning around the school. The pony behaved so well that Ellie quickly became more ambitious. "Trot on," she called out.

Shadow leaped forward eagerly into a bouncy trot while Ellie pounded along behind him. Shadow trotted faster and faster. Ellie struggled to keep up, but it was hard work running in the sand of the ring.

She was just about to tell him to walk again when she tripped and fell flat on her face.

The fall knocked the wind out of her, but she managed to hold on to the reins. Shadow felt a pull and stopped. He turned his head around curiously to see what Ellie was doing.

Meg ran over and took hold of his bridle, while Kate helped Ellie to her feet. "Well . . . he handled that all right," Meg said. "But maybe next time we'll practice where it's easier to run."

"Let's use the park," said Ellie, as she brushed the sand from her clothes. "You can't see it from the palace, so no one will discover our secret before we're ready."

With that agreed on, Ellie and Kate put Shadow away and headed to the workshop to start fixing up the carriage. Kate's granddad was already there waiting for them. He patiently showed them how to rub down the peeling woodwork and paint on new varnish.

"You'll need to wear something old," he said to Ellie. "That varnish will ruin those nice clothes of yours."

"But I don't have anything old or gross," she replied. "Princesses don't have old clothes."

So, for the next few days, Ellie worked on the carriage wearing a pair of Kate's granddad's coveralls with the sleeves and pants rolled up.

Except for taking care of her ponies, it was the nearest she had ever come to real work. Varnishing was a whole new experience, and so was vacuuming the old cushions to get rid of the dust.

When they weren't working on the carriage, the two girls continued with Shadow's lessons. The Shetland thrived on all the attention and was soon happily pulling a log.

"He's doing really well," said Meg on the Tuesday afternoon before Great-Aunt Edwina was due to arrive. "He's ready for his big test, as soon as the carriage is finished."

"It looks fantastic," said Ellie. "It should be all set by tomorrow."

Unfortunately, Kate's granddad didn't agree. "Those wheels are still a bit stiff. I've got to do some more work on them and check the whole thing over to make sure it's safe. It'll be ready the day after tomorrow and not a minute earlier."

Ellie pleaded with him, but he wouldn't

change his mind. So Shadow's first real drive was set for Thursday morning. Ellie knew that that was cutting things very close. The pony was being picked up on Friday. This would be Shadow's one and only chance to prove himself as a driving pony. They couldn't afford to have anything go wrong.

Chapter 8

By Wednesday evening, Ellie was feeling super nervous. What if the carriage weren't ready? What if Shadow hated pulling it? What if her parents were so angry with her for going behind their backs that they insisted on selling him anyway?

She was forced to push her panic aside when Great-Aunt Edwina's ancient car roared up the palace drive. Ellie and her parents waited to greet her at the main entrance, while a nervous footman ran down the steps to open the car door.

Great-Aunt Edwina stepped out, looking regal in a long skirt and velvet cape. She glanced disapprovingly at the footman. "Dear, dear," she said. "Servants always looked so much nicer when I was a girl."

"Here we go again," muttered the King under his breath.

Ellie knew what he meant. She just hoped that her great-aunt's arrival wasn't going to spoil her secret plan. There were already enough things that might go wrong.

Luckily, the weather wasn't one of them. Thursday morning was perfect for Shadow's big day. The sky was blue, the birds were singing, and sunlight glittered on the distant sea.

Ellie put on her jeans and the only T-shirt she had that wasn't pink. Then she headed for the stable. But when she was only halfway down the main hall, she heard the unmistakable voice of Great-Aunt Edwina.

"Aurelia, Aurelia," she called, spying the princess. Then she glanced disapprovingly at Ellie's clothes and added, "Oh, my. Princesses never wore pants when I was a girl."

"They do now," said Ellie, as firmly as she could without being impolite.

"Your dear parents are a little busy this morning," said her great-aunt. "They said they were sure you would be happy to keep me company."

Ellie smiled weakly. Her *dear* parents had obviously already had enough of their difficult relative. Now it was her turn to suffer. Worse still, it meant there was no chance of Ellie getting to the stable in time to get Shadow ready. She stopped a passing maid and sent her to the stable with a message saying she would meet the others in the park. Then she led Great-Aunt Edwina to one of the largest of the palace sitting rooms while she desperately tried to figure out a way to escape from her great-aunt.

"What shall we do?" asked  Edwina, as she settled herself in a red velvet chair.

Ellie ignored the "we" and pulled a pack of cards from a desk drawer. "You could play solitaire," she suggested. Great-Aunt Edwina could play that by herself, so she wouldn't need Ellie's company.

"Nonsense," said the old lady. "We need something we can do together. Go and get the chess set."

Ellie sighed and did as she was told. The card trick had not worked, but she was determined not to give up. She couldn't bear the thought of sitting inside all morning while the biggest event in Shadow's life was happening somewhere else.

It was hard to concentrate on chess with so many thoughts racing around her brain. Was the carriage ready? What was Shadow doing? Most important of all, how was she ever going to escape from Great-Aunt Edwina?

Three long games later, she still hadn't thought of a plan. She was also convinced that *nothing* made her great-aunt happy.

"You've lost again, Aurelia," said Great-Aunt Edwina, without seeming at all pleased to have won. "Maybe you don't practice enough. When I was a girl, your dear grandmother and I used to play every day."

The mention of her grandmother made Ellie remember the two little girls smiling in the photograph in the royal album. "I saw a picture of both of you the other day," she said. "You must have been very young—only five or six, I think."

"It would be interesting to see that," said Great-Aunt Edwina.

Ellie's eyes twinkled mischievously as she had an idea. "Come with me," she said. "I am sure my governess would be delighted to show you. She has lots of pictures."

Ten minutes later, Ellie was on her way to

the park, leaving Great-Aunt Edwina discussing the good old days with Miss Stringle. Ellie glanced down anxiously at her watch as she ran. She was very late. "I hope they haven't started without me," she thought out loud. "And I really hope nothing else goes wrong today."

Chapter 9

Ellie reached the park just in time. Kate was holding Shadow, while her granddad helped Meg get the carriage into position, with one shaft on either side of the pony.

"Ellie—you're here! I'm so glad!" said Kate. "We thought you weren't going to make it."

"So did I for a while," said Ellie. "Great-Aunt Edwina nearly ruined everything. She wanted to play cards!" She walked over and helped lift the shafts through the leather loops, called tugs, on each side of the harness. Then she hooked one of the long leather traces to her side of the carriage, while Meg hooked on the other one.

"The traces are what Shadow actually pulls the carriage with," explained Meg, as she adjusted the last few straps on the harness. "The shafts are only there to make him go straight."

Shadow had stood perfectly still while all this was going on, but now he stamped one tiny hoof impatiently on the ground.

"I think he wants to get started," said Meg with a laugh. She gave Shadow a pat, climbed up into the carriage, and took hold of the reins. "You two, walk beside him for a while, just to make sure everything is okay."

She told Shadow to walk on, and he moved forward willingly. Ellie was surprised at how easily the carriage rolled after him. Kate's granddad had worked wonders on the wheels.

Shadow behaved perfectly as they practiced stopping, starting, turning, and trotting. He even walked backward a few steps when Meg told him to. But best of all, he seemed to be enjoying himself. He held his head proudly, with his neck arched and his ears pricked forward.

Eventually, Meg stopped him and told Ellie and Kate to get into the carriage with her. "He's a great driving pony," she said. "There's no need for you to walk beside him anymore."

The carriage swayed slightly as they climbed in. Ellie was surprised at how different it felt from a car. The big wheels were designed to give a smooth ride, but it still bounced as it rolled along.

As soon as Ellie got used to the feel of it, Meg swapped places with her so that she could drive. Ellie felt very proud and slightly scared as she picked up the reins. Shadow was a long way in front of her, and there was

no one there to grab him if anything went wrong.

"You'll be fine," said Meg, reassuringly. "Just do what we've been practicing all week."

Ellie's nerves rapidly calmed down once they started moving. Soon, she was confident enough to ask Shadow to trot. It was a wonderful feeling driving along in the carriage. There was no noisy engine as there would have been in a car—just the sound of the wheels turning and Shadow's hooves pounding on the ground.

"Let's go somewhere," suggested Kate. "It'd be more fun than just going around and around the same patch of grass."

The idea appealed to Ellie. She turned Shadow on to a gravel path lined with tall

trees
on either side.
Their branches
met high in the air,
forming a tunnel of green.
"We'll still be safe here," she said. "No one
can see us from the palace."

Shadow's hooves crunched on the gravel
as he trotted along. The sun glinted through
the leaves, making patches of light on the
ground. It was peaceful and quiet. The only
sound was the *clop-clop* of Shadow's hooves
and the rustling leaves. The tunnel felt like a

magical place—a place where almost anything could happen.

Unfortunately, something did.

When they rounded the next bend, they
came face to face with Great-Aunt Edwina.

Chapter 10

Ellie's heart sank as she pulled Shadow to a halt. Trust Miss Stringle to mess things up, she thought. She must have persuaded Great-Aunt Edwina to go for a walk.

"What are we going to do?" whispered Kate.

Ellie had no idea. She wanted to be the one to show Shadow's secret to her parents. She didn't want her grumpy great-aunt spoiling the surprise by moaning about it in advance. Then Ellie realized that, for the first time ever, Great-Aunt Edwina was smiling.

"What a dear little pony," said the old lady, as she stroked Shadow's nose. He seemed to approve of the attention and nuzzled her long skirt, searching for treats. "He's just as sweet as the one I had when I was a girl."

Ellie was amazed. Great-Aunt Edwina looked very different when she smiled. "Would you like to go for a ride?" Ellie asked her. "There's plenty of room for four."

The old lady's smile grew even broader, and her eyes twinkled as she climbed into the carriage. "What I'd really like to do is drive," she said. "I used to love driving when I was a girl."

Ellie was amazed. This was a whole new Edwina! Ellie shuffled closer to Meg to make room on the seat. Then she handed her great-aunt the reins. The old lady took them expertly and soon had Shadow on the move again. At the end of the tree-lined path, Great-Aunt Edwina turned him toward the palace.

"No!" shouted Ellie and Kate at the same time.

"Why not?" asked Great-Aunt Edwina. "I haven't had this much fun since I was a girl. We'll have to show your parents."

Ellie tried to explain about the secret, but there wasn't time. Before she had finished, they were driving up to the royal garden, where the King and Queen were sitting in their outdoor thrones, relaxing in the sun.

"What is going on?" asked the King, jumping to his feet in astonishment. The movement dislodged his crown, which slipped sideways over one eye.

The Queen stood up in a more dignified manner. "Where did that carriage come from?" she asked. "And what's Shadow doing pulling it?"

The King pushed his crown straight and looked at Ellie suspiciously. "Have you been up to something, Aur—?"

"Isn't it wonderful?" interrupted Great-Aunt Edwina. "I'm really enjoying myself."

The King and Queen stared at her in amazement. They had never seen their grumpy relative look happy.

"I'm so pleased," said the Queen.

"And I'm so surprised," added the King in a very quiet voice.

Great-Aunt Edwina winked at Ellie. "I do

hope I'll be able to do it again," she said sweetly.

"So do I," said the Queen. "It's lovely to see you enjoying yourself so much."

Ellie got down from the carriage. "Does that mean we don't have to sell Shadow?"

The King looked doubtful. "I don't know. It's certainly exciting that Shadow can pull a carriage. But there's still the problem of his health."

"You don't have to worry about that anymore," said Meg, helpfully. "Now that we can drive him, he'll have plenty of exercise."

"So can he stay?" pleaded Ellie.

"Hmmm," said her father, thoughtfully. Then he glanced at Great-Aunt Edwina and smiled. "I don't know what you've been up to in secret, Aurelia, but it seems to have worked out for the best. You may keep Shadow."

"And I should think so, too," said Great-Aunt Edwina. "We never got rid of perfect driving ponies when I was a girl."

Ellie was so relieved that she nearly burst into tears. She threw her arms around Shadow's neck and hugged him. "You're safe now," she said. "You can stay here for ever and ever."

Here's a sneak peek at the next adventure
of the

Pony-Crazed
Princess

in

Princess Ellie's
Mystery

Princess Ellie's Mystery

Chapter 1

"Let's explore," said Princess Ellie, as she stopped Rainbow at the entrance to the woods. The path was a long, dark tunnel. On one side was a high brick wall. On the other, trees grew so close together that their branches arched overhead and shut out the sun.

"Are you sure?" said her best friend, Kate. The palomino she was riding fidgeted, shifting her weight from foot to foot, her golden coat gleaming in the sunshine. Moonbeam was the most nervous of Ellie's four ponies.

"Yes," said Ellie. She wasn't ready to go back to the palace yet. When she was there, she had to be Aurelia, not Ellie. She had to follow rules and behave like a proper princess. Out here, she was free to do as she liked.

Ellie squeezed with her legs, and Rainbow stepped forward obediently. Kate followed close behind on Moonbeam.

"It's spooky in here," said Kate nervously, as they rode into the shade of the trees.

"Don't be silly," laughed Ellie. "Surely you don't believe in ghosts." Riding Rainbow gave her confidence. The gray pony was brave and reliable.

It was very quiet in the woods. There were no birds singing, and the path was covered with a thick, springy layer of rotting leaves that muffled the sound of the ponies' hooves.

As they rode deeper and deeper into the woods, Ellie looked around at the moss-covered wall and the damp tree trunks. Kate was right, she thought: it was a little spooky in there.

She pushed the gray pony into a trot, eager to reach the sunshine on the other side as quickly as possible.

Rainbow now seemed uneasy, too. She tucked in her head and blew down her nose nervously.

Suddenly, Rainbow stopped. Ellie was

taken completely by surprise, and she shot forward in the saddle. Rainbow didn't give Ellie time to recover her balance. Instead, the gray pony spun around on the spot, trying to head back the way they had come.

Ellie swung sideways. She felt herself slipping and tried to grab hold of the saddle. But she had already gone too far.

She was going to fall off.

To find out what happens next, read

Princess Ellie's Mystery